"Here," Ray said. "Sit in my chair." He pushed James into his chair.

James laughed and twisted around in the chair. "What are you doing?"

"For today, you're Ray," Ray said. "And I'm James."

"What?" James said.

Ray went down the aisle and sat at James's desk. "Hi, Ray," Ray said.

James started to laugh. "Hi, James," he said.

"How are things up there, Ray?" Ray asked.

"Not bad, James," James said. "How are things back there?"

"Boring, Ray," Ray said.

The classroom door opened, and a woman with a black brief-case stepped inside. "Good morning," she said. "I'm Mrs. Walters. Mr. Hart is sick today."

James looked back to see if Ray wanted to change seats. But Ray was stretched out in James's chair with a big smile on his face.

OTHER PUFFIN CHAPTERS YOU MAY ENJOY

The SUB

P.J. Petersen

illustrated by Meredith Johnson

PUFFIN BOOKS

PUFFIN BOOKS
Published by the Penguin Group
Penguin Putnam Books for Young Readers,
345 Hudson Street, New York, New York 10014, U.S.A.
Penguin Books Ltd, 27 Wrights Lane, London W8 5TZ, England
Penguin Books Australia Ltd, Ringwood, Victoria, Australia
Penguin Books Canada Ltd, 10 Alcorn Avenue, Toronto, Ontario, Canada M4V 3B2
Penguin Books (N.Z.) Ltd, 182-190 Wairau Road, Auckland 10, New Zealand

Penguin Books Ltd, Registered Offices: Harmondsworth, Middlesex, England

First published in the United States of America by Dutton Children's Books,
a division of Penguin Books USA Inc., 1993
Published in Puffin Books, 1995
Reissued 2000

1 3 5 7 9 10 8 6 4 2

Text copyright © P. J. Petersen, 1993
Illustrations copyright © Meredith Johnson, 1993
All rights reserved

THE LIBRARY OF CONGRESS HAS CATALOGED THE DUTTON EDITION AS FOLLOWS:
Petersen, P. J.
The sub / by P. J. Petersen; illustrated by Meredith Johnson.
1st ed. p. cm.
Summary: Two friends switch seats when their class has a substitute teacher
and find that it isn't so easy to be someone else.
ISBN 0-525-45059-9
[1. Schools—Fiction. 2. Substitute teachers—Fiction. 3. Friendship—Fiction.]
I. Johnson, Meredith, ill. II. Title.
PZ7.P44197Su 1993 [Fic]—dc20 92-22269 CIP AC

This edition ISBN 0-14-130709-9

Printed in the United States of America

For my friend Joe Vargas

P.J.P.

The
SUB

1

James was playing catch with his best friend, Ray. The first bell was about to ring, and the playground was crowded. Kids were playing tetherball and wallball and four-square.

Ray was joking around, the way he always did. He put his baseball glove on top of his head. Then he held his cap out in front of him. "Toss the old potato in the bucket," he called.

James laughed and threw the ball. Ray reached out with his cap but missed the ball. "I need a bigger hat," he said.

James looked toward the teachers' parking

lot. Mr. Hart was late. Most mornings, he would stop and play catch with them for a minute. For a grown man, Mr. Hart wasn't a very good ballplayer. But he always made them laugh. He threw his Super Curve Ball, which didn't curve, and his Super Drop Ball, which didn't drop. And he opened his briefcase and used it to catch the ball.

James wasn't a very good ballplayer either, but he had fun playing with Ray. Ray was always making jokes. James could never think of jokes, but that didn't matter. Ray had enough jokes for the whole school.

"Hey, sleeping beauty, wake up!" Ray yelled.

James turned and saw the ball coming straight at him. He jumped out of the way. The ball hit the ground and rolled away.

Ray let out a laugh. "We're not playing dodge ball."

James ran after the ball and picked it up. "Just a second," he called. He saw Mr. Luna's old blue truck chugging into the parking lot. Mr. Luna and Mr. Hart rode to school together.

Mr. Luna got out of the truck alone. "Hi, Mr. Luna," James called. Mr. Luna waved to him. "Where's Mr. Hart?"

"He's sick," Mr. Luna said. "You'll have a substitute today."

James felt cheated. School wasn't the same without Mr. Hart. "Mr. Hart is sick," he yelled to Ray, then threw the ball—hard. Ray had to jump high to catch it. "This is going to be a rotten day," James said. "I hate having a sub."

"Maybe we'll get movies all day," Ray said. "That's what the sub did last year, remember? Six hours of movies. We all went home with big old red eyes." He threw the ball to James.

The ball bounced off James's glove and hit

him in the chin. That's the kind of rotten day it was going to be.

When the first bell rang, James and Ray headed for their classroom. Ray put the ball in his cap and put the cap on his head. Blake was inside the door with the ball box. Ray took off his cap and let the ball fall into the box. Blake checked off their names.

"We have a sub today," James told him.

"Did you see that game last night?" Blake said. "The Rams got smashed."

James walked to his desk. Amy sat across from him. As usual, she was writing a letter. "We have a sub today," James told her.

"Maybe he'll be cute," Amy said. "The sixth graders had a really cute sub last week." She began to fold her letter. She always folded her letters into little tiny wads.

James looked back at Paul. Paul had the desk right behind his. Paul was drawing a motorcycle on the cover of his math book. While he drew, he went "*rroom-rroom*" like a motorcycle. "We have a sub," James told him.

"Teachers are lucky," Paul said. "I wish I could stay home and send a sub in my place."

James lifted the lid of his desk, then slammed it down. There was no reason to get out his books. Not with a sub coming. Everything would be different today. Different and rotten. And he was the only one who cared.

James went up the aisle. Ray's desk was two desks ahead and one desk over. Ray was standing by his chair. He had his baseball glove on his head again.

"Maybe they can't find a sub," James said.

"I hope they do." Ray opened the lid of his desk, bent down his head, and let the glove fall onto the piles of papers. "If they can't find somebody, we get the principal."

"I'd rather have the principal than a sub," James said. "The subs don't even know who you are. All they do is look at the seating chart. If we changed seats, the sub wouldn't even know. You'd be James, and I'd be Ray."

Ray broke into a smile. "That's a great idea."

James looked at him. "What do you mean?"

"Here," Ray said. "Sit in my chair." He pushed James into his chair.

James laughed and twisted around in the chair. "What are you doing?"

"For today, you're Ray," Ray said. "And I'm James."

"What?" James said.

Ray went down the aisle and sat at James's desk. "Hi, Ray," Ray said.

James started to laugh. "Hi, James," he said.

"How are things up there, Ray?" Ray asked.

"Not bad, James," James said. "How are things back there?"

"Boring, Ray," Ray said.

"Hey, James," James called, "can I borrow a pencil?"

Ray opened James's desk. "No problem, Ray. I have a whole bunch." He tossed James a pencil. "Nice catch, Ray."

The classroom door opened, and a woman with a black briefcase stepped inside. "Good morning," she said. "I'm Mrs. Walters. Mr. Hart is sick today."

James looked back to see if Ray wanted to change seats. But Ray was stretched out in James's chair with a big smile on his face.

Right away, Mrs. Walters took out the seating chart and called roll. When she called Ray's name, everybody looked at James. "Here," James said. Everyone smiled.

When Mrs. Walters called James's name, Ray said, "Present." Some of the kids laughed out loud.

While Mrs. Walters took care of lunch money, people kept smiling at James. "Hey,

Ray," Blake whispered to James, "you must have gone on a diet. You're smaller than you were yesterday."

James liked the way people smiled at him. For once, he was in on the joke. It was going to be a good day after all.

2

James had never had a sub like Mrs. Walters. He couldn't help liking her. She was a big, friendly woman with a happy laugh. Her dress hung almost to the floor. She had on floppy sandals that poked out below the dress. When she walked, the sandals went *blip-smack, blip-smack*.

Most subs acted lost at first. Not Mrs. Walters. She started a lesson right away, showing them old pictures of their town. The pictures were taken before cars were invented. Then she made them list good things and bad things about living back then. Everybody's first answer for bad things was "No TV." So she made them think of good things about not having TV.

That was hard. People looked at each other and shook their heads. "There aren't any," Ray said.

Mrs. Walters laughed. "Keep thinking," she told them.

"I could get more sleep on Saturday mornings," Blake said. "I wouldn't have to get up early to watch cartoons."

"That's a start," Mrs. Walters said.

James raised his hand. "Maybe families would talk more," he said.

Mrs. Walters glanced at the seating chart. "Good answer, Ray."

Everybody smiled again.

At recess, James and Ray checked out a ball and played catch. "Mrs. Walters is okay,"

James said. "But I still wish Mr. Hart wasn't sick."

"I don't care what she says," Ray said. "There's nothing good about not having TV."

Other kids came around and wanted to play with them. "Throw me the ball, James," they said to Ray.

"Nice catch, Ray," they said to James.

James loved every minute of it.

After recess, Mrs. Walters had them write down things that they saw in the fall. Then she wrote their answers on the board to make one long class poem. Most people said things like "falling leaves" and "pumpkins" and "Halloween."

Sara said, "Ice on my horse's water trough."

Paul said, "New shows on TV."

And Blake said, "The World Series."

"This is a great poem," Mrs. Walters said.

"But we still have a little room on the board. Let's finish with some really happy things. Write down something that you love doing in the fall."

For a minute, James couldn't think of anything. Then he thought about raking leaves with his dad. What James loved to do was get a big pile of leaves and then run and jump right in the middle of it. He loved to hear the leaves snap and crunch. And he loved to sink into the pile.

He grabbed his pencil and wrote: *Jumping into a big pile of leaves*.

On the board, Mrs. Walters had written: WE LOVE . . . She smiled and said, "Okay, what do we love?" Lots of people raised their hands.

Tim said, "Building a fire in the fireplace."

Ann said, "Making a jack-o'-lantern."

Blake said, "Pigging out on trick-or-treat candy."

James waved his hand in the air. He was smiling. In his mind, he saw himself jumping into a pile as big as a house.

Mrs. Walters turned toward the class. "James?"

"Jumping into a big pile of leaves," James called out.

At the same time, Ray shouted, "Watching 'Monday Night Football.' "

The class broke out laughing.

James slid down in his desk. He felt really stupid. He'd forgotten he was sitting in Ray's seat.

Mrs. Walters looked straight at him. "I said *James*. I'll take you next, Ray." She looked at him for a long time, then turned and wrote Ray's answer on the board. Then she looked back at James. "Yes, Ray?"

"Jumping into a pile of leaves," James said quietly.

Mrs. Walters filled the whole board. Then

she stood back and read the long poem. "What a great poem," she said. And she read it again.

James kept his eye on Mrs. Walters. She was watching him. He was sure of it. But when her eyes moved his way, he looked down. He wondered if Mrs. Walters knew he wasn't Ray. But if she did know, why didn't she say something? He wondered what she'd do if she found out. Take him to the principal? Send him home?

If she was going to do something, James wished she'd hurry up and do it.

"I think she knows," James told Ray at lunch.

"No way," Ray said. "If she knew, we'd be out of there."

"She keeps looking at me funny."

"She's probably just looking at the rip in your shirt," Ray said.

James looked down at his shirt. "What rip?"

Ray poked him and laughed. "Gotcha."

Amy came over to them and said, "You boys are going to get in big trouble."

"If you tell on us," Ray said, "we'll tell about all those dumb letters you write."

Amy smiled. "I won't tell. But somebody might." She went skipping across the playground.

"That's the worst thing about your desk," Ray said. "Every time I look up, I see that brat's face."

When they went back inside, James walked right past Ray's desk. Ray grabbed his shoulder. "Where are you going, Ray?" he said.

"I forgot," James said. He slid into Ray's desk. He wished he didn't have to sit there. That desk didn't feel right. Not at all.

Mark's desk was right behind his. Mark kept kicking James's chair. Not hard. Just little taps.

"Stop that," James said.

"Stop what?" Mark asked.

"You're kicking my chair."

"Oh," Mark said. But thirty seconds later, he was kicking the chair again.

"You're kicking the chair," James said.

"Don't be such a grouch," Mark said.

Sara sat down in the desk to James's left. She leaned across the aisle. "Do me a favor," she said. "When Blake comes in, tell him my little sister thinks he's cute."

"Tell him yourself," James said.

"Just give him the message," Sara said. "Ray always does it for me."

"I'm not Ray," James said.

"For today you are," Sara said.

Blake ran into the room just as the bell rang. He was almost to his seat by the time the bell stopped.

Sara reached over and tapped James. "Go ahead."

"Not right now," James said.

"Please," Sara whispered.

James glanced toward the front desk. Mrs. Walters was taking papers out of her brief-case. He leaned toward Blake and whispered, "Sara's little sister thinks you're cute."

Blake waved him away. "Get outa here. Sara's sister is a stupid pest. I wish she'd move to Antarctica and take Sara with her."

Sara smiled. "I think he really likes her," she told James.

Mrs. Walters looked down at her chart. "Sara, Ray. No talking."

James sighed. He was tired of being Ray. And Mark was kicking his chair again.

3

The last class of the day was reading. Mrs. Walters began by reading them the first few pages of some books. She always stopped right in the middle of a good part. "Read some more," everybody said.

"You get to read the rest yourself," Mrs. Walters said. "And it gets better and better." Then she picked up another book.

Afterward, Mrs. Walters said they would have silent reading. "Mr. Hart says that you each have a book to read."

James opened Ray's desk. It smelled funny. Like old tuna fish. Very old tuna fish. He dug

through all the crumpled-up lunch bags and wadded-up papers to find Ray's book. It was a really easy book about a horse. James had read the book when he was in the first grade. And it wasn't very good then. He opened it up. It smelled like tuna fish, too.

And Mark was kicking James's chair again.

James reached down and tapped Mark's foot. "What?" Mark said, but he quit kicking.

After James had read a few pages, he heard Ray whispering: "Ray. Hey, Ray."

James looked over his shoulder. Ray pointed to the book he had taken from James's desk. Then he held his nose.

James gave him a disgusted look. That book was about explorers going to the North Pole. It was a great book.

"It stinks," Ray whispered. It was a whisper that the whole class could hear. "It's a rotten book."

"That's enough," Mrs. Walters said. She

went to the blackboard and wrote *James Parker* up in the corner.

James could hardly keep from yelling. That wasn't fair. He hadn't done anything, and his name was on the board. Mr. Hart would come back tomorrow and see it. And he'd think James had made trouble for the substitute.

James looked down at his smelly horse book. He hoped Ray didn't make any more trouble. If he did, James would get checks after his name. One check was a warning. But if you got two checks, you had to stay in at recess. With three checks, you got a note to take home. Four checks sent you to the principal.

What if Ray thought this was funny? What if he started talking and laughing back there? James could end up taking a note home. Or going to the principal.

James glanced back at Ray. Ray wasn't even reading. His book was closed. He was looking up at the ceiling. Now James was really worried. Ray could never sit still for very long.

James knew what would happen next. First, Ray would look around. Then he'd yawn and stretch. Then he'd look over at somebody's book. If it looked good, he'd ask to read it next. And just about then, James would get a check after his name.

James glanced at Mrs. Walters. She was sitting on Mr. Hart's desk. She was reading their science book. Her floppy sandals were hanging from her toes.

James looked back at Ray. Ray was yawning. He stretched his arms high in the air.

James had to do something. In another minute, Ray would start to talk to somebody.

"Ray," he whispered. Ray didn't look at him. "Ray."

Amy reached over and tapped Ray. "Huh?" Ray said. Amy pointed at James.

"Be careful," James whispered. "Don't get me in trouble."

"Turn around in your seat, Ray," Mrs. Walters said. She slid off the desk and went to the blackboard. Right below *James Parker*, she wrote *Ray Nelson*.

"Good," Blake whispered. "That'll pay him back."

James looked over his shoulder. "I didn't mean to," he whispered.

Ray pointed a finger at him. "I'll get you for that," he whispered. Then he smiled. But it wasn't a good smile.

Mrs. Walters walked back to her desk. James looked down at his stupid horse book. He wanted the day to be over. He just wanted to go home and play with his dog and forget about school.

BOOM!

James spun around. The noise sounded like a firecracker. People started to laugh the way they do after they've been scared. Then James saw Ray pick up his book from the floor.

"Sorry," Ray said. He didn't sound sorry at all.

Mrs. Walters marched to the blackboard. "The next person to drop a book wins a free trip to the principal's office," she said. Then she put a check after James's name.

"That's not fair," Blake whispered to James.

James looked back at Ray. Ray pointed at him and smiled.

So Ray had done it on purpose. He was paying James back.

James was angry. He had a check after his name. And Ray was sitting back there smiling.

It was a bad way to treat a friend. Ray wasn't his friend at all. No friend would get you in trouble that way. And no friend would smile about it afterward.

If Ray was going to act like that, James could do the same. But he had to be careful. He looked up at the clock. Fifteen minutes to go.

He'd be quiet for now. Then, just before the bell rang, he'd make noise and get a check. And it would be too late for Ray to pay him back.

"Ray," Sara whispered. "Hey, Ray." She had a note on the edge of her desk. She wiggled it up and down.

James waved her away.

Sara wiggled the note. "Take it."

"Put away the note, Sara," Mrs. Walters said. She got up and wrote Sara's name on the board.

"It's your fault," Sara whispered to James. "If you'd taken the note, I wouldn't be in trouble."

James looked down at the horse pictures in his book. At the bottom of the page was a red blob. It looked like strawberry jam. James put his finger on the blob to see if it was sticky. It was.

James glanced up at the clock to see how much time had gone by. Only two minutes. He counted to a hundred before he looked at the clock again. Then he counted to a hundred once more—slowly. Mark started kicking James's chair again. James counted the kicks.

When the clock showed one minute to go, James got ready. He had to time things just right. Twenty seconds before the bell, he'd start talking—loud.

But Mrs. Walters slid off the desk and said, "All right. Put your things away."

James hadn't planned on that. But he started talking just the same. "This is a stupid book," he said. "It's the worst book I ever read."

Mrs. Walters smiled at James, but she didn't walk to the board.

"This book is worse," Ray shouted. "It stinks!"

Mrs. Walters kept smiling. "Thank you for

sharing that," she said just as the bell rang.

Ray came running up the aisle. "I know what you were doing, you sneak," he said to James. "You were trying to get me when it was too late for me to get you back. And it didn't work, did it?"

"And who slammed his book on the floor?" James said.

"And who's got a check after his name?" Ray said. "And it serves you right." He pushed past people and ran out of the room.

James shook his head and walked to the door. "Good-bye, Ray," people called to him. And "See you later, Ray." They were all smiling.

James didn't feel like smiling. Not with Ray mad at him and not with his name on the blackboard with a check after it. That's the first thing Mr. Hart would see tomorrow.

Mrs. Walters was standing by the door.

"Good-bye, Ray," she said. "Maybe I'll see you again sometime."

James waved, but he didn't say anything. He hoped he never saw Mrs. Walters again in his whole life.

4

James didn't sleep very well. And he woke up long before his mother knocked on his door. He was sure somebody would tell Mr. Hart. Then Mr. Hart would take James aside and ask, "What do you have to say for yourself?" (That's what Mr. Hart always asked.) And what could James answer?

On the bus ride to school, James sat by himself and looked out the window. He kept wondering what Mr. Hart would do. Last year, a sixth grader had been kicked out of school for a week. Would they do that to James?

And what about Ray? Would he still be mad?

James hated fighting. He was ready to be friends again—if Ray was. But what if Ray didn't want to be friends.

Before James stepped off the bus, he wondered if Ray was playing ball with somebody else. Then he saw Ray waiting for him. "Hey, James," Ray said, "let's go play catch. I already got the ball." Ray lifted his cap to show the ball sitting on his head.

James smiled and took his glove out of his backpack. Ray made things easy. They didn't have to explain and say they were sorry or anything. They could just forget about what had happened and go play ball.

He wished things could be that easy with Mr. Hart.

Ray and James walked past the tetherball games to the far side of the playground. "It'll be good to get back to my old desk today," Ray said.

That surprised James. Why would anybody

want to move from James's great desk back to one stuffed full of old papers and lunch bags? "What's wrong with my desk?" he asked.

Ray smiled. "Don't get mad," he said. "I just can't stand it back there. Old Amy's got her nose into everything. And Paul is playing motorcycles. And your desk is so clean. It's like the dentist's office."

James didn't think his desk was anything like the dentist's office. He had his things right where he wanted them, that's all. But he didn't want to argue about it. He set his backpack on a bench and said, "Throw me the ball."

"Here comes a coconut out of the tree," Ray said. He threw the ball high in the air. James held his breath. He had trouble with high ones. He was always afraid high ones would hit him in the head.

But this time the ball smacked into his glove. And it stayed there. He'd caught the first ball. It was going to be a good day.

Ray pounded his fist into his glove. "Let's see your fast ball. Burn it in here."

James pitched the ball. His fast ball wasn't very fast. But Ray acted like it was. He caught the ball and spun all the way around. "Faster than a speeding bullet," he yelled.

James looked over at the parking lot. Mr. Luna's truck was there. So Mr. Hart was already inside. "Hey, Ray," James said, "you think we ought to tell Mr. Hart what we did?"

Ray laughed. "Oh, sure. And let's tell the principal, too."

But James was serious—even if the idea was a little scary.

He wasn't scared of being punished. Unless they got kicked out of school. And James didn't think that would happen. They'd probably have to stay in for recess. Or maybe pick up papers at lunchtime.

Those things wouldn't be so bad. The hardest thing would be telling Mr. Hart.

"Here you go," Ray called. "Another co-conut." He threw the ball high into the air. James backed up until he was right under it. The ball came down and hit James's glove. Then it bounced off and hit his chest. But he grabbed the ball before it fell. So it was still a catch. Not a great catch, but a catch.

"I mean it, Ray," said James. "If we don't tell Mr. Hart, somebody else will. And then we'll really get it."

Ray shook his head. "If we tell him, we'll get it anyway."

"Let's do it," James said. "I want to get it over with."

Ray looked at him. "Are you sure?"

"Pretty sure."

"Okay," Ray said. "Then let's do it before everybody gets in there."

James grabbed his backpack, and they walked toward the room. "How do we get started?" James asked.

"This was your idea," Ray said. "You do the talking."

"I need a drink of water," James said. He stopped at the drinking fountain and took a drink. Then he took another one. "Come on, Ray. What do I say first?"

Ray smiled. "Just say, 'Good morning, Mr. Hart.' "

James took another drink. "You know what I mean. I need a way to get going. I don't want to stand there like a dope." He looked down at the fountain. He couldn't hold any more water.

"We could tell him we're sorry," Ray said.

"I'm sorry," James said quietly. "I'm sorry." That sounded all right. Maybe it wasn't a great start. But it was a start.

James hurried toward the room. Ray ran along beside him. "I'm sorry," James whispered. "I'm sorry."

When they got to the door, Ray stepped in front of James. He grabbed the doorknob. That was fine with James. He was happy to let Ray go first.

But Ray pulled open the door and held it for James. James stopped for a second, then stepped through and opened his mouth. He wanted to start talking right away. "I'm—" he began.

Mrs. Walters looked up from the desk. "Well, hello, Ray. And James. Hello, boys. How are you this morning?"

5

James stared at Mrs. Walters. His mouth stayed open, but no more words came out.

Mrs. Walters smiled at him. She asked him something, but he didn't hear what she said. He looked back at Ray. Ray was standing there with his mouth open.

"You're early," Mrs. Walters said. "The bell didn't ring, did it?"

"No," James said quietly. She wanted to know why they were there. But James couldn't think of a reason.

After a minute, Ray said, "Ray wanted to put away his backpack."

James felt much better. "Yeah," he said quickly. Good old Ray had saved him. He hurried toward his desk. But for a second, he forgot he was Ray. He walked right past Ray's desk.

"Hurry up, Ray," Ray called out.

Then James remembered. So he turned around and hurried back up the aisle. He shoved his pack under Ray's chair and headed for the door.

As soon as they were outside, Ray started laughing.

"It's not funny," James said. "I just about gave us away."

But Ray kept laughing. "You should have seen your face."

"Listen," James said. "We've got to be really careful today. No trouble. No checks. All right?"

"I'll try," Ray said.

"Don't try," James said. "Do it."

When the bell rang, James and Ray went back into the room. That time, James went straight to Ray's desk and sat down. The first thing he noticed was the smell. He opened the lid and looked inside.

The same old lunch sacks were in there. And crumpled papers. And candy wrappers. And paper towels. And sandwich bags. Inside one of the sandwich bags was an apple core, covered with blue mold. It looked like a blue worm. A hairy blue worm.

James slammed down the lid of the desk. It was going to be a long day.

Mark came down the aisle. "Hi, Ray," he said. He sat down and started kicking James's chair.

"Take this, Ray," Sara said. She handed him a note. "Put it on Blake's desk."

The note wasn't folded at all. James couldn't help reading it:

MY SISTER LIKES YOU.

DO YOU LIKE HER?

__YES   __NO   __MAYBE

When Blake saw the note, he took out a black marker pen. He crossed out YES and MAYBE. Then he put a big check by NO. Then he drew a circle around NO. Then he wrote a big black NO on the whole paper. At the bottom he wrote:

P.S. SHE MAKES ME SICK!!

P.P.S. SO DO YOU!!!!

"Give this to her," Blake told James.

James handed the note to Sara. She looked at it and smiled. "I don't think he means it," she said.

Mrs. Walters showed them more pictures from the early days. Then she read from old letters people had written back then. The letters talked about games that kids played. And the work they did around the house. One girl wrote about riding her horse into town to buy groceries.

"Wow," Sara said. "Riding a horse to the store. I wish I could be back there."

James wished he could be back there, too. In fact, he wished he could be anywhere but at Ray's desk.

Mrs. Walters gave them special homework. They were each to talk to an older person. They were to ask the older people what they did when they were kids. Tomorrow each student would give an oral report.

James raised his hand and asked, "If Mr. Hart comes back, will we still give the reports?"

"Good question, Ray," Mrs. Walters said. "Mr. Hart won't be back until Thursday at the earliest."

James looked down at his desk. Two more days of being Ray. Two more days to watch what he said and did. Two more days to wonder if somebody was going to tell on him. James didn't think he could stand it.

They had to read in their social studies books for the rest of the period. James got out Ray's book and opened it. The book smelled like peanut butter. That was better than tuna fish, anyway.

James read two pages. Then he looked up. Mrs. Walters was sitting on her desk, watching him. He was sure of it. Maybe somebody had told on him. Maybe Mrs. Walters knew he wasn't Ray. But if she did, why didn't she say something?

James looked down at his book. He wished the clock would move faster.

"There's a bumblebee on the ceiling," Ray said out loud.

Everybody laughed and looked up.

Mrs. Walters slid off the desk and put another check besides James's name.

"That's not fair," Ray said. "I was just warning you."

Mrs. Walters smiled. "If you'd been reading, you wouldn't know what was on the ceiling."

After that, everybody kept looking up at the bee. The bee didn't do anything interesting. In fact, it didn't do anything at all. It just sat in the same spot. But everybody watched it—just in case.

James looked up at the bee, too. But he also looked at the board and at the checks after his name. James was mad. He really wasn't mad at Ray. He knew Ray hadn't done it on purpose. But the checks were there just the same.

A few minutes later, Mark tapped James on the shoulder. James glanced back. Ray held up a paper. It had two big words written on it: I'M SORY.

"You didn't spell it right," Amy said.

Mrs. Walters walked over and wrote Amy's name on the board.

That was the only good thing that happened that morning.

6

After recess, Mrs. Walters passed out a test on math facts. James didn't know what to do. If he took a test for Ray, that was cheating.

Besides, Ray wasn't good at numbers. When he added, he still used his fingers.

Maybe they could change papers when they were done. If they were careful, maybe Mrs. Walters wouldn't see them.

The test was easy. James did all of the problems, then checked each one. He found one mistake and corrected it.

He glanced over his shoulder. Ray was bent

over his paper. His nose was about an inch from the desk.

James stared at the top of Ray's nose. Somebody had told him that if you stared that way, the other person would look up.

It didn't work. Ray kept his eyes on his paper. Every once in a while, he put down his pencil and counted on his fingers.

Mrs. Walters came down the aisle. Her sandals went *blip-smack* with each step. She stopped beside James. "Face the front," she said quietly.

James hoped she didn't think he was trying to cheat. "I'm done," he said.

Mrs. Walters smiled at him. "Not quite."

"I checked them all," he said.

"Yes, but you didn't put your name on your paper."

James picked up his pencil and wrote *Ray* at the top.

Mrs. Walters looked over his paper. "Good job, Ray. I don't see a single mistake."

After the test, they went to the gym for music. Every Tuesday at ten-thirty, Mr. Lamb taught singing. Usually James didn't like singing. He didn't like sitting on the floor with four other classes. And he didn't like the way Mr. Lamb always stopped them right in the middle of the song. "Let's try that again," he'd say. Over and over again.

But today James was happy to go to music. For a whole period, he didn't have to be Ray.

When they came back from music, Mrs. Walters handed them their tests. "Good work, Ray," she told James. At the top of his test was *100%* and a smiling face.

She handed Ray his test. "Keep working on these," she said. "It just takes practice."

A minute later, Mark tapped James on the shoulder.

James leaned back, but he didn't turn around. He didn't want to get a check by Ray's name.

"James," Mark whispered, "Amy says to tell you that you missed seventeen."

"Seventeen?" James said at lunch. "How could you miss seventeen?"

Ray laughed and gave him a shove. "What do you mean? I got a hundred percent. You're the one who missed seventeen."

"Big joke," James said.

"Come on," Ray said. "I didn't do it on purpose. I just didn't finish."

"You could have asked for more time," James told him.

Ray stopped smiling. "I didn't want to look stupid."

"So *I* end up with the bad grade," James said.

"I hate this," Ray shouted. "I hate being you. I hate having to be so careful. And I hate Mrs. Walters. And, worst of all, I hate that Amy. She sneaked a look at my paper, and then she told the whole world."

Kids on the playground looked at them. James stared at Ray. It always surprised him when Ray got mad. "It's okay, Ray," he said. "One bad grade won't kill me." He tried to sound happier than he really felt.

"Right," Ray said. Then he laughed. "If bad grades could kill you, I'd have been dead a long time ago."

After lunch, Mrs. Walters sat on the desk and read poems to them. Funny poems about having ice cream run down your chin. And about an octopus playing baseball. And one about a man with a pumpkin for a head.

Then she had them write their own poems. She had a special kind. First they put down their name. Then two words to tell about themselves. Then they described themselves doing three things. And they finished with their name again.

Mrs. Walters wrote this poem about herself:

Mrs. Walters.
Busy. Hungry.
Watching students.
Thinking about a snack.
Waiting for the bell.
Mrs. Walters.

When James started his poem, he put *James* at the top. But then he remembered. He stopped for a minute. It was harder to write a poem about Ray. James wanted a good poem about Ray. But he didn't want it to sound like bragging. After all, he was Ray. Sort of.

He got another paper and wrote this poem:

>Ray.
>
>Happy. Funny.
>
>Telling jokes.
>
>Running on the playground.
>
>Catching a baseball.
>
>Ray.

When Mrs. Walters asked people to read their poems, James's hand shot up into the air. When he read his poem, people smiled. "Good poem, Ray," Blake said.

A minute later, Mrs. Walters called on Ray. Ray had a big smile on his face. He stood up and read this poem:

>James.
>
>Neat. Smart.
>
>Cleaning his desk.

Petting his dog.
Dreaming of girls.
James.

Everybody in class roared. Everybody but James. Ray took a bow and sat down. James was furious. How could Ray do that to him?

Other kids read their poems. But James didn't listen. He kept looking back at Ray.

And Ray just sat and smiled.

After school, Ray came running up to James. "I made it," he said. "I went the whole afternoon and didn't get a check after your name. I thought I was going to die back there, but I didn't say one word."

"You made me look stupid," James said.

Ray stepped back. "What are you talking about?"

"That poem," James said. "Saying I dream about girls. Why'd you do that?"

"Come on," Ray said. "I was just having a little fun. Besides, *I'm* James, remember?"

"It was a rotten thing to do," James said.

"Why do you have to worry so much?" Ray said. "It was just a joke."

"It was a stupid one," James said.

Ray shook his head. "I hate this," he said. "Everything I do, I have to worry about you. I keep quiet all afternoon, and you're still not happy. I hate it."

"Well, I have to worry about you, too," James said. "And I hate it as much as you do."

7

On Wednesday morning, James decided not to go to school. He didn't want to sit at Ray's desk again. He didn't want to pretend to be Ray.

It would be nice to stay home for a day. He could read books and play with his dog and watch a little TV. Later on, he could build something with his Lego blocks.

"I'm really sick today," he told his mother.

"I'm sorry to hear that," his mother said. Right away, she took his temperature. He didn't have a fever.

"What hurts?" she asked.

James couldn't think of a good answer.

So he ended up on the bus.

It should have been a good day. On Wednesday, his class got an hour of sports with Mr. Sanchez. That was always fun.

And James had done a good job on his homework. He had a great report to give.

He'd talked to his neighbor, Mr. Clark. Mr. Clark had told him about games he used to play like run sheep run and red rover. He used to mow his neighbors' lawns with a mower that didn't have a motor. And he only got paid twenty-five cents. But candy bars and soda pop only cost five cents then.

But it wouldn't be James's report. It would be Ray's.

"No," James said out loud. The people on the bus turned and looked at him.

James didn't care. He'd had enough. It was time to end the stupid joke.

When James got off the bus, he saw Ray waving a ball. "Let's go," Ray called.

James walked over to him. "I tried to stay home today," James said. "But my mom didn't believe I was sick."

"Mr. Hart better come back tomorrow," Ray said. "If I have to be back there with old Amy much longer, I really will be sick."

"I'm sick now," James said. "Even if my mother doesn't think so."

Ray slapped him on the back. "Just one more stupid day."

"I can't stand one more day," James said. "Let's go in and tell Mrs. Walters right now."

Ray looked at him and laughed. "Oh, sure."

"I mean it," James said. "Let's go tell her."

"That's crazy," Ray said. "She'll send us right to the principal."

"I don't think so," James said. "Not if we say we're sorry."

"There's one little problem," Ray said. He flapped his arms and went "Cluck, cluck."

"I'm not chicken," James said.

"Maybe not," Ray said. "But I am. Cluck, cluck, cluck."

"Let's do it," James said again.

"All right," Ray said. "But you do the talking."

James headed straight for their classroom. Ray stayed one step behind him.

"You really don't think she'll send us to the principal?" Ray asked.

James didn't answer. He didn't want to think about the principal. He walked right past the water fountain. His throat was dry, but he didn't want to stop.

James pulled open the door and held it for Ray. But Ray grabbed the door and pushed James into the room.

Mrs. Walters was sitting at her desk. She

glanced up once and said, "Hi, Ray. Hi, James." Then she went back to her papers.

James walked toward her desk. He had to hurry before he got too scared. "Mrs. Walters," he said quickly.

She looked up at him and smiled. "Yes, Ray?"

James stood and looked at her. In his mind, he saw the door to the principal's office. "Well, uh," he said. That wasn't much of a start. "Well, see, uh."

"What is it, Ray?"

James didn't say anything for a minute. Then Ray poked him in the back. "I have something—" he began.

The door banged open. "Mrs. Walters!" Amy yelled. "Mrs. Walters! Carmen tore her dress playing two-square. She stepped on the hem, and the whole thing ripped."

"Where is she?" Mrs. Walters asked.

"She's in the rest room. She ran in there right away. She had to. You could see her slip and everything."

Mrs. Walters opened a desk drawer and took out her purse. "I'll be there in just a second," she said. "We'll fix it."

"I'll tell her you're coming," Amy said. She ran out the door.

Mrs. Walters stood up. "Did you boys have something you wanted to tell me?"

James looked down at his feet. "That's okay. It doesn't matter."

"Carmen can wait," Mrs. Walters said.

James couldn't think of the words. "No, that's okay."

"Ray just wanted to put away his backpack," Ray said.

Mrs. Walters grabbed her purse and started for the door. But she stopped and turned back to them. "Are you sure?"

"It's okay," James said.

Once Mrs. Walters was gone, James walked over and slammed his backpack onto Ray's desk.

"Cluck, cluck," Ray said.

"I didn't hear *you* say anything," James said.

Ray laughed. "I told you I was chicken before we started."

James kicked the desk. "I just stood there like a dope."

"It's okay," Ray said. "Let's go play catch."

James got his glove and kicked the desk again. He hated being Ray. But he didn't like being stupid, scared James either.

When the bell rang, they walked back to the classroom. "Who did you talk to for your report?" James asked.

"I was going to talk to my grandma," Ray said. "I tried to phone her, but she wasn't home."

James grabbed Ray's arm. "So what are you going to do?"

Ray pulled away. "Quit worrying so much. I'll just tell Mrs. Walters what happened. It's not my fault my grandma wasn't home."

"And you'll get a zero for me," James said. "That's not fair."

Blake came up beside them. "What's not fair?"

"Ray didn't do a report," James said.

"It wasn't my fault," Ray said.

"No problem, Ray," Blake said. "Just make up something. That's what I'm going to do."

"What?" James said.

Ray laughed. "See, James? No problem."

James shook his head. He knew what was going to happen. Ray would give a rotten report. And James would get the rotten grade.

It served him right. He'd had his chance to tell, but he'd been too scared.

Mrs. Walters started the day by showing them ads from old newspapers. Then she asked for their reports. James looked up at the clock. They had twenty minutes until recess. Maybe she wouldn't get to Ray.

The reports were interesting. Tim had a top that his grandfather had played with. Tim tried to spin it for the class, but it didn't work very well.

Amy told about a game called jackstraws. And Paul had a toy train that was over sixty years old.

But the reports went by too fast. When nobody else raised a hand, James raised his. He told everything he could think of, but his report still didn't take very long.

"That's very interesting, Ray," Mrs. Walters said.

Then nobody had a hand up. Mrs. Walters began calling on people. Blake was first. He stood up and said, "I talked to an old guy down the street."

"What was his name?" Mrs. Walters asked.

Blake's face turned red. He looked down at his feet. "I forget."

"Go ahead," Mrs. Walters said.

"He played, uh, baseball and, uh, jack-straws." Blake kept looking at the floor. "That's all, I guess." He flopped down in his seat.

James glanced back at Ray. Ray looked scared. Now Ray knew it wasn't so easy just to make up something.

"James?" Mrs. Walters said.

Ray started to stand up. Then he shook his head. "I was going to talk to my grandma," he said. "But she wasn't home." He looked at James for a second. "I'm sorry, Mrs. Walters. I'll talk to her today."

Mrs. Walters smiled and put a mark in her book. James knew what that mark was. A big zero.

James felt like screaming. He was mad at Ray. Ray should have tried harder. He could have talked to somebody else.

But mostly, James was mad at himself. He should have told Mrs. Walters the truth when he had the chance.

Sports hour was the period before lunch. Their class was the only one outside. Mr. Sanchez took the softball players, and Mrs. Walters took the volleyball players.

James was happy to be on the softball field.

"How's it going, James?" Mr. Sanchez asked.

"Fine," he said. It really did feel fine to be James again.

James's team was out in the field first. James was playing second base. He smacked his fist into his glove. "Let's get an out," he yelled.

Mr. Sanchez pitched. He threw the ball easy, so everybody could hit. The first batter struck out, even with Mr. Sanchez's easy pitches. James felt sorry for him.

Ray was the next batter. He waved the bat over his head. "This one's going over the fence," Ray yelled.

James hoped Ray would get a hit. Ray was on the other team, but that didn't matter. And he was mad at Ray for not doing a report, but that didn't matter either. Ray was his baseball pal, and he wanted Ray to smack one.

Ray hit the first pitch hard. The ball came right at James. He didn't have time to catch it. He didn't even have time to duck. The ball hit him in the chest and bounced to the ground.

"Get the ball," somebody yelled.

James saw the ball by his foot. Ray was running toward first base. James picked up the ball and threw it hard to the first baseman.

It was a close play. Ray saw the ball coming and took one last long step. His foot landed on the side of the base, then twisted. Ray went tumbling to the ground.

"He's out," somebody yelled.

"Safe," somebody else yelled.

James saw the look on Ray's face and yelled, "He's hurt." James ran toward Ray. Ray lay in the dirt, holding on to his ankle.

Mr. Sanchez came running, too. "Don't move, Ray!"

Ray looked up and tried to say something, then shook his head.

James dropped to his knees beside Ray.

"Take it easy, Ray." He put his hand on Ray's shoulder. He could feel Ray's whole body shaking.

Mr. Sanchez squatted down and checked Ray's foot and leg. All the others crowded around.

"Is it broken?" Paul asked.

"Shut up, Paul," somebody said.

James looked down at Ray. Ray had his eyes closed and his jaw locked tight. Tears were running down his cheeks. James wiped away the tears. It had been a long time since he had seen Ray cry.

"Okay, Ray, put your arm around my neck," Mr. Sanchez said. "I'm going to carry you inside." He got his arms under Ray and stood up.

"Don't drop me," Ray said and smiled for a second.

Mr. Sanchez took a few steps. "This guy's

heavy." He looked at James. "Run to the cafeteria and get some ice."

James went running. The cook gave him a plastic bucket half full of ice.

By the time James had gotten the ice, Mr. Sanchez and Mrs. Walters had Ray sitting in a chair outside the main office.

While Mr. Sanchez filled the bucket with water, James and Mrs. Walters took off Ray's shoe and sock. "Don't tickle my toes," Ray whispered.

James tried to smile, but he didn't feel like laughing. Ray's ankle was twice its usual size.

Mr. Sanchez and James helped Ray lift his foot into the bucket.

"That's cold," Ray said.

"That's the whole idea," Mr. Sanchez said. He looked at Mrs. Walters. "You'd better call his parents. See if they can take him to the doctor."

"Sure," Mrs. Walters said. She started into the office.

James felt better. Ray's ankle was in ice water, and soon he'd be at the doctor's.

But then it hit him—Mrs. Walters was about to go and call *his* mother. And Ray needed help right now. "Oh, no!" James shouted. He ran for the office.

"What's the matter?" Mr. Sanchez asked.

James raced through the door. He didn't care what happened to him, as long as Ray got help.

Mrs. Walters was just picking up the phone. "Mrs. Walters," James shouted, "*he's* Ray Nelson. Not me. We've been playing a joke."

Mrs. Walters punched the numbers on the telephone. Then she smiled at James. "I know," she said.

After phoning Ray's father, Mrs. Walters went back to the playground. James and Mr. Sanchez stayed with Ray.

James wanted to talk to Ray about Mrs. Walters. But Mr. Sanchez was right there. He told them riddles and stupid jokes. Jokes like "Ray's mom calls him Sonny because he's so bright."

Ray smiled now and then, but he didn't seem to be listening. Once he looked up at James and asked, "Was I out or safe?"

"I think you were safe," James said.

"You were out," Mr. Sanchez told him. "Out of luck."

Ray's father came just after the lunch bell rang. He looked scared. "Don't worry, Dad," Ray said. "I'll be all right in a few years."

Mr. Sanchez carried Ray to the car, and James carried the bucket. Ray's father held the door open for them. Then he took the bucket from James.

After Ray's father drove away, James asked Mr. Sanchez, "You think he'll be all right?"

"Ray'll be fine," Mr. Sanchez said. "I'm not so sure about his dad."

James walked back to the classroom. Everybody else was outside eating lunch. He'd be able to see Mrs. Walters alone.

He felt rotten. But in one way, he felt better. At least he didn't have to pretend anymore.

He pulled open the classroom door. Mrs. Walters was sitting at her desk. "How's Ray?" she asked.

"His dad took him to the doctor," James said. Then before she could say anything, he went on. "I'm sorry. It was stupid. It was a joke, and then we couldn't stop."

"I know," Mrs. Walters said. She had her hand in front of her mouth. She almost looked like she was laughing.

"I tried to tell you, but then I got scared," James went on.

Mrs. Walters nodded and turned her head away.

"How did you find out the truth?" he asked.

Mrs. Walters turned to look at him. She opened her mouth, then shook her head and broke out laughing. She leaned back in her chair and laughed and laughed. James didn't know what to think. He was glad she wasn't angry. But he didn't understand why she was laughing.

"Oh, James," she said in a minute, "I'm sorry. I'm not laughing at you. But I've been

holding back all week." She broke out laughing again. "You remember that first morning when we were doing our poem? I called your name, and both of you answered."

James didn't think it was very funny. "So you knew right away?"

"I knew something wasn't right," she said. "You two had such funny looks on your faces. And every time I called one of your names, the whole class laughed. So I checked your files at lunch. Your picture's in the file, you know."

"But—" James started. He stopped because he didn't know what to ask.

"I called Mr. Hart right then," Mrs. Walters said. "He said I should pretend I didn't know. He said you and Ray might learn something."

"We did," James said. "Was Mr. Hart mad?"

Mrs. Walters smiled. "A little. But he knows

everybody does dumb things once in a while." She looked at James and laughed again. "Oh, James, I wanted you to tell me this morning. You came so close."

"I'm sorry," James said.

"You said that already." Mrs. Walters looked at James. "Now what? What does Mr. Hart do with people who make mistakes?"

"Sometimes they have to write papers, saying what they did wrong. And sometimes they pick up litter at lunch hour."

"Those sound good," she said. "Which one is right for you?"

"Both," James said. He grabbed the wastebasket and headed for the playground.

After lunch period, James came back into the room. He set the wastebasket beside Mrs. Walters' desk. "Ray's father just called," she said. "Ray has a bad sprain, but he'll be fine."

"Good," James said, then shook his head. "I don't mean it's good that he has a sprain. I mean—"

"I know what you mean," Mrs. Walters said.

"When will he be back at school?" James asked.

"Tomorrow, if he feels all right," Mrs. Walters said. "But he'll have to take it easy."

"I'll help him," James said. He turned and walked down the aisle, right past Sara and Mark. He was headed for his own desk—with no tuna fish smell. And no horse book. And no moldy apple cores.

"I told you you'd get in trouble," Amy said.

James just smiled. Amy was a pain sometimes, but today she didn't bother him at all.

Paul was drawing something on the back of his hand. Probably a motorcycle. He was going "*rroom-rroom*" while he drew.

"Hi, Paul," James said.

"Hey," Paul said. He kept on drawing.

James kept smiling. At least Paul never kicked James's chair.

James sighed as he slid into his seat. It was very, very comfortable.

P. J. PETERSEN has spent many years in school—first as a student and now as a teacher. Mr. Petersen is the author of numerous books for young readers, including *I Hate Camping*, *I Hate Company*, and *The Fireplug Is First Base*. He lives in Redding, California.

MEREDITH JOHNSON has illustrated many children's books, among them *Soccer Shock*, by Donna Jo Napoli, and *Can You Keep a Secret?*, by P. J. Petersen. Ms. Johnson lives in Pasadena, California.